To Mila, for transforming life into a beautiful tale.
José Carlos Andrés

To Isabella, my little mouse.
Betania Zacarias

Every time a child loses a tooth, a little someone takes it and leaves a small gift in return.

While in France, Spain and South America it is a small mouse, in England and the United States it is the Tooth Fairy.

In other countries, it is an angel or even a squirrel.

The Untold Story of The Tooth Fairy
Somos8 Series

www.nubeocho.com – info@nubeocho.com

Original title: *La primera aventura del ratoncito Pérez*
English translation: Robin Sinclair
Text adaptation: NubeOcho
Text editing: Caroline Dookie and Ben Dawlatly

Distributed in the United States by
Consortium Book Sales & Distribution

First edition: 2017
ISBN: 978-84-944446-1-6
Printed in China

THE UNTOLD STORY OF THE TOOTH FAIRY

JOSÉ CARLOS ANDRÉS   BETANIA ZACARIAS

Are you ready to hear about the **origin** of the **Tooth Fairy?**

It is said that **she was an oyster** who lived in the deep sea. I know it sounds **weird,** but let me start from the beginning.

A long time ago, something happened at the **bottom of the sea,** at the very deepest depths...

Lady Oyster was very very sad, because she had lost her only pearl. She wailed nonstop in her opera singer's voice:

"Oh, I am very, and I mean very, so very sad, because I have lost my only pearl.

Oh, I'm just so upset!"

Lady Oyster told a nice, slow **octopus** from the deeper depths what had happened to her, as he dragged himself along the bottom of the sea:

"Friendly octopus dragging yourself across the bottom of the sea, I am very, and I mean very, so very sad because I have lost my only pearl.

Oh, I'm just so upset!"

The **octopus** (the one who lived in the deepest depths of the sea and was slower than a clock without batteries), told a **French sardine** who was swimming nearby what had happened to Lady **Oyster**:

"Listen, Sardine, Lady Oyster is very, and I mean very, so very sad, because she has lost her only pearl."

The **sardine** (the French one, who was swimming nearby), told the story to an eight-legged **crab** who was moving fast toward the sea shore:

"Monsieur crab, Madame Oyster is sad, so very sad, so extraordinarily sad, because she has... she has lost her only pearl."

And the **crab** (the one with so many legs who was in such a hurry) told the story to a little **mouse** who was taking a stroll on the sandy beach:

"Heyheyhey little mouse, Lady Oyster is veryveryvery but veryveryvery sad because she has lost her only pearl."

And the **little mouse,** moved by these words, decided he had to help Lady Oyster. He thought that the best solution would be to find something to replace the lost pearl.

It would have to be something
small, white, hard and shiny.
Like a **pearl**.

The **little mouse** began his search and he found a **button** that was small, white, and shiny... but it wasn't very hard... The mouse could easily crack it with his sharp **teeth.**

He kept searching and he found a **stone** that was hard, white and small... but it wasn't shiny.

That wouldn't work either!

He searched a bit more and he found a very special **coin,** which wasn't white but it was very shiny and very hard... although it was too large to fit inside an **oyster.**

The little mouse liked the **shiny** coin and decided to keep it, even though he didn't know how he would use it.

And that was when, searching and searching, the little mouse entered a little girl's room, whose tooth had fallen out that day. She had placed it beneath her **pillow.**

The little mouse saw the **tooth** and grabbed it, because it was small, white, hard, and shiny:

"This will be perfect!" the little mouse cried.

And **in exchange** for taking the **tooth,** the little mouse decided to leave underneath the **little girl's pillow** the only thing he had: the shiny coin that he had found.

He would have liked to have left her a **book,** but he didn't have one with him at the **time.**

The little mouse ran toward the **beach** to deliver the tooth to the **crab**, who when he saw it, shouted:

"Yesyesyes! This will be perfect! Yesyesyes!"

And the crab gave it to the sardine, who shouted:

"Oh la la! C'est parfait!"

And the sardine gave it to the octopus, who shouted:

"This will be perfect!"

And the octopus delivered the tooth to Lady Oyster who, as soon as she saw it and examined it closely, shouted... **Do you know what she shouted?**

"This is perfect!"

She was so very pleased and **thanked them all**.

This is how Lady Oyster became the **Tooth Fairy** and the mouse, the octopus, the sardine and the crab became her **secret assistants**.

And every time a child **loses a tooth,** the Tooth Fairy knows and the little mouse carries away the tooth and gives it to the crab, who gives it to the sardine, who gives it to the octopus, who gives it to the **Tooth Fairy.**

And in exchange for the tooth, they leave a **small gift** for the child.